SIZZLING Celebrities

Adele!

SINGING SENSATION

BY ALLY AZZARELLI

Enslow Publishers, Inc.
40 Industrial Road
Box 398
Berkeley Heights, NJ 07922
USA
http://www.enslow.com

Dedicated to Jaime H., an Adele fan

Library of Congress Cataloging-in-Publication Data:

Azzarelli, Ally.

    Adele! : singing sensation / by Ally Azzarelli.
       p. cm. — (Sizzling celebrities)
   Includes index.
   Summary: "Read about Adele's early life, how she got started in music, and her future plans"—Provided by publisher.
   ISBN 978-0-7660-4172-1
   1. Adele, 1988—Juvenile literature. 2. Singers—England—Biography—Juvenile literature. I. Title.
   ML3930.A165A99 2014
   782.42164092—dc23
   [B]

                2012040311

Future editions:
Paperback ISBN: 978-1-4644-0283-8
EPUB ISBN: 978-1-4645-1178-3
Single-User PDF ISBN: 978-1-4646-1178-0
Multi-User PDF ISBN: 978-0-7660-5807-1

Printed in the United States of American

062013 Lake Book Manufacturing, Inc., Melrose Park, IL

10 9 8 7 6 5 4 3 2 1

To Our Readers: We have done our best to make sure all Internet addresses in this book were active and appropriate when we went to press. However, the author and the publisher have no control over and assume no liability for the material available on those Internet sites or on other Web sites they may link to. Any comments or suggestions can be sent by e-mail to comments@enslow.com or to the address on the back cover.

 Enslow Publishers, Inc., is committed to printing our books on recycled paper. The paper in every book contains 10% to 30% post-consumer waste (PCW). The cover board on the outside of each book contains 100% PCW. Our goal is to do our part to help young people and the environment too!

Photo Credits: AP Photo/Alison Wise, p. 9; AP Photo/Chris Pizzello, pp. 26, 31; AP Photo/Donn Jones, p. 23; Photo by Evan Agostini/Invision/AP, p. 35; AP Photo/Joel Ryan, pp. 24, 33; AP Photo/Jonathan Short, File, p. 29; AP Photo/Keystone/Sandro Campardo, p. 18; AP Photo/Mark J. Terrill, pp. 20, 22, 27; AP Photo/Matt Dunham,p . 16; AP Photo/Matt Sayles, p. 14; AP Photo/Peter Kramer, p. 40; AP PHOTO/Remy de la Mauviniere, p. 7, Chris Pizzello/Invision/AP, p. 46; John Shearer/Invision/AP, p. 1; Photo by Evan Agostini/Invision/AP, p. 39; Photo by Jordan Strauss/Invision/AP, pp. 4, 8, 38; Press Association via AP Images, p. 10; PRNewsFoto/Columbia Records, p. 44.

Cover Photo: John Shearer/Invision/AP (Adele poses with her award for best original song for "Skyfall" during the 2013 Oscars.)

Contents

A Star Is Born

Who would think three songs on a Myspace page could make a girl famous? Not Adele! And, it wasn't even her idea to post them. She has a friend to thank for that. Adele made a demo as a class project. A demo is a sample of different songs. Adele's friend created the Myspace music page for her on New Year's Eve 2004.

Within a year, e-mails from record labels came into Adele's inbox. She thought it was a prank or Internet hoax. She had never heard of a record company called Island or XL—two of the record labels that contacted her. At first she ignored their messages. Then, after her mom insisted, she returned a call. She met with a representative from XL. The label signed her on the spot.

Moving Around

Adele Laurie Blue Adkins was born May 5, 1988, in Tottenham, North London. It was a poor area. Many people didn't have jobs. The crime rate there is twice as high as it is for England.

◀ *Adele looks at her award for Best Original Song in a Motion Picture for Skyfall at the 70th Annual Golden Globe Awards on January 13, 2013.*

Her mom had many jobs. She was a masseuse (someone who gives massages), furniture maker, and office worker. Adele's parents lived together until she was three. Then her dad moved out. Her mom has always been there for her. "She's a great mum. She's always been supportive. She's my best friend," Adele told *People* magazine.

Adele and her mom moved around a lot. When she was nine, they moved to Brighton; at ten, to Brixton; and then to neighboring West Norwood, in South London, which later became known in her hit "Hometown Glory." They didn't have a lot of money. They often lived in government-paid housing. But this didn't stop Adele from dreaming. Adele's mom told her she could be whatever she wanted. But her mom also said she should keep her options open.

Music Roots

A fan of music at a young age, Adele enjoyed singing for her mom's friends when they visited. Her mom would gather lights together, like stage lights. Adele would feel like she was in the spotlight. Adele liked singing Spice Girls songs. The Spice Girls are an all-girl English pop group. They were popular in the mid-'90s. In 2012, they made a comeback, inspiring a musical and performing at the closing ceremony of the Summer Olympics. Adele especially loved Mel B, also known as Scary Spice. Adele considers the Spice Girls a major inspiration. She started listening to them when she was seven. "I love the Spice Girls because they made me who I am," she told Nowmagazine.com.

The British girl group the Spice Girls was a major inspiration for Adele.

Gabrielle, a fellow Brit singer from London, is also a role model for her. Gabrielle is known for her style and fashionable eye patch. She sings jazz and rhythm and blues. Gabrielle has a lazy eye. Although Adele didn't have an eye condition, her mom made her a sequined eye patch so she could look like Gabrielle!

Adele's early inspiration also came from Etta James, Ella Fitzgerald, Peggy Lee, and Jeff Buckley. She also likes Aaliyah, Mary J. Blige, Lauryn Hill, Alicia Keys, and Beyoncé. Adele's

◄ *Adele knew she wanted to be a singer after seeing P!nk in concert.*

most memorable concert was when she saw P!nk. "It was the Missundaztood record, so I was about 13 or 14," Adele told Spinner.com. "I had never heard, being in the room, someone sing like that live . . . . I remember sort of feeling, like I was in a wind tunnel, her voice just hitting me. It was incredible," she said of P!nk's Brixton Academy concert. The concert made a big impression on Adele. She knew around that time, age fourteen, that she wanted to be a singer.

Adele fell in love with the jazzy, bluesy music she's known for when she was shopping for a new hairstyle. She was going through the sale bin at British record store HMV. Looking for hairstyle ideas on the covers, she came across albums by Etta James and Ella Fitzgerald. "[Etta James] was the first time a voice made me stop what I was doing and sit down and listen," Adele told *Rolling Stone.* "It took over my body."

And to think, when Adele came across her first Etta James album, she had no idea who she was. She loved how Etta looked. She just loved her style! "I bought the record not knowing anything about her . . . . didn't listen to it for ages, and then a couple years later—at 15, and everything was changed."

"There was no musical heritage in our family," Adele told the *Telegraph* in a 2008 interview. "Chart music was all I ever knew. So when I listened to the Ellas and the Ettas . . . . it was like an awakening. I was like, 'Oh right, some people have [long careers] and are legends.' I was so inspired that as a 15-year-old, I was listening to music that had been made in the 40s." She discovered the difference between singers who have the quick No. 1 hit, and those who are around a long time. Their music becomes a part of history.

Etta James was a major inspiration for Adele. Here, James performs at the Vine St. Bar & Grill in Hollywood in 1987.

During Adele's secondary school, or junior high, she met kids who liked R&B music. She would sing with her new friends on the playground. Adele joined the choir. Having a teacher helped perfect her singing. Her school required her to play an instrument. She chose the clarinet. She realized she preferred singing. She then found a school that allowed her to focus on singing—her true love!

Dan Smith and Shingai Shoniwa of the Noisettes arriving for the Sony Radio Academy Awards 2010. Shingai inspired Adele to write her own music.

School Days

By the time she was fourteen, Adele had been singing and playing the guitar and clarinet for years. Adele auditioned for London's BRIT school, a performing arts high school. Her mom supported her all the way. Other artists, such as Amy Winehouse, Leona

Lewis, Jessie J, and Kate Nash also went to the school. "It was like *Fame*," she told *Rolling Stone*. "There were kids doing pirouettes in the hallway and doing mime, and having sing-offs in the foyer." *Fame* is a television show from the early 1980s about a performing arts high school in New York. Some compare it to today's popular show *Glee*.

Adele loved that her performing arts school had free rehearsal rooms and free equipment. "I was listening to music all day, every day for years." The experience was great. Her music classes were the real deal. "She was an ordinary teenager who had a special talent. There were no artificial airs about her. She got to where she is through sheer hard work," BRIT teacher Arthur Boulton told *People* magazine.

By her second year in the performing arts school, she found inspiration. That's when Shingai Shoniwa, vocalist for the Noisettes, became her neighbor. Adele thought Shingai was an amazing singer. She would listen to her singing through the walls. Shingai inspired her to write songs. Before she met Shingai, Adele was only singing songs written by other people.

Lesson Learned

Adele had one weakness when it came to school: she wasn't always on time. "I'd turn up to school four hours late. I was sleeping, I wasn't doing anything . . . . I just couldn't wake up." That all changed the day that she was late for a class field trip.

Teachers had picked twenty of the best students to perform at a festival.

Adele slept too late that morning. She felt awful when she realized she missed the trip. She had been so excited for it too. Oversleeping that day almost got her kicked out of school. Since then, Adele is rarely late for things.

Her Big Break

Adele's big break came during her last year at BRIT in 2006. A friend had posted three of Adele's songs on Myspace on New Year's Eve 2004. Adele had recorded the songs as part of a class project. Within about a year, she was talking to a record label. XL is home to other acts popular in the UK, including M.I.A., The Prodigy, and Radiohead.

Adele's Journey

Adele met with XL's Nick Huggett in June 2006. He told manager Jonathan Dickins at September Management about Adele. Later that month, Dickins became Adele's manager. This is someone who helps plan a singer's career.

This was great news for Adele. September Management was also managing Jamie T, a fellow Brit singer and songwriter. Adele was a huge fan of Jamie T. In September 2006, Adele was signed to XL. When she signed with XL Recordings, she "thought it would be an underground London thing, not a worldwide thing," she told a reporter for People.com. Soon after, Adele sang vocals for Jack Penate's song "My Yvonne." While helping with this song, Adele met producer Jim Abbiss, who would later be a bigger part of her life. A producer is someone who perfects an artist's recordings and music.

Hometown Glory

Adele's first hit, "Hometown Glory," debuted on October 22, 2007. She wrote this song in 2004, when she was sixteen.

◄ *Adele poses for a portrait in Los Angeles in 2008.*

The song came to her quickly. She was inspired by the idea of going off to Liverpool. Adele and her mom fought. Her mom wanted her to go, to be able to grow on her own. Adele wanted to stay in London, where she was comfortable and knew her surroundings.

The song was released on a 7" vinyl single, which is a 45-rpm record. Before compact discs and iTunes, people listened to recorded music on audio cassette tapes and record players. A 7" vinyl record played on a record player moves at a speed of 45 rpms, or rotations per minute. Only five hundred copies were made. It was released on Jamie T's Pacemaker Recordings label. The song failed at first. But the week her album *19* was released in January 2008, fans flocked to buy the song once it was available for download. It was the first single released from the album.

All About *19*

Adele's song "Chasing Pavements" was the second single and was released on January 11. The song came out two weeks before the album's debut. "Chasing Pavements" climbed to the #2 spot on the UK charts, where it stayed for four weeks.

"Chasing Pavements" was written after Adele found out a boyfriend had cheated on her. "I went to the pub [where he was] and punched him in the face," Adele told *Rolling Stone.* "I got thrown out . . . . As I was running away, the phrase 'chasing pavements' came to me." On the way home, she recorded the lyrics into her phone.

Adele titled her album *19* after the age she was when she recorded the songs for the album. *19* debuted at number one on the British charts when it was released on January 28, 2008.

Adele's third hit from *19*, "Cold Shoulder," came out in March 2008. March 2008 also brought Adele another record deal with XL.

Columbia Records prepared her CD for its U.S. release later that year. (Sometimes, a different record company will release a British singer's album in the United States after it has already been released in Great Britain.) She began a short U.S. tour in

◄ *Adele performs at the BRIT Awards in 2008. She won the Critics' Choice Award.*

March for a couple of months, with *19* released in the United States in July.

Around the time *19* came out, Adele met someone. British actor and singer known as Slimy Slinky Winfield, or Slinky Sunbeam, was from a resort town in England. He also later became the inspiration for her next album, *21*. He was ten years older than she was. He made her feel like an adult. He helped her stop and take a look at her life. "Most of my life was my career, but I had this little side project that was us. And it made me feel really normal again, which is just what I needed. Because I was becoming a bit . . . . crazy," she told *Rolling Stone*.

Her An Evening With Adele tour began in May and ended in June. Later that year, the singer made the covers of gossip magazines. She canceled sold-out U.S. tour dates of her An Evening With Adele tour. Fans were shocked and saddened. She was deeply in love at the time. Looking back, she realized this was not smart. She told *Nylon* magazine, "I couldn't bear to be without him, so I was like 'Well OK, I'll just cancel my stuff then' . . . . I can't believe I did that . . . . It seems so ungrateful."

In July 2008, Adele's version of Etta James's "Fool That I Am" appeared on the B-side of her rerelease of "Hometown Glory." It was from a live concert in Cambridge, England. The tune was to be her first release in the United States. At that time, it was Adele's third UK Top 20 hit!

"Hometown Glory" on TV & With Other Artists

In the winter of 2008, "Hometown Glory" was featured on popular television shows. Her song could be heard on episodes of *Skins*, *One Tree Hill*, *Grey's Anatomy*, *Hollyoaks*, *So You Think You Can Dance*, *The Hills*, and even a number of UK and U.S. soap operas.

TV shows weren't the only ones picking up on the success of "Hometown Glory." Fellow singers started sampling Adele's lyrics within their own music. Mississippi rapper Big K.R.I.T.'s "Hometown Hero," Big Sean's "Hometown," French rapper La Fouine's "Vecu" featuring French rapper Kamelancien, OCS's "Hometown," and Minneapolis artist Mod Sun on the song "Same Way" all did so.

Here, Adele sings during the 42nd Montreux Jazz Festival in Montreux, Switzerland, on July 12, 2008.

America Loves Adele

By October 2008, it looked like Adele wasn't going to make it in the United States. That was until she was the musical guest on *Saturday Night Live*. This episode featured actor Josh Brolin, and had a special appearance by Sarah Palin. At that time, Sarah Palin was a U.S. vice presidential candidate from Alaska. Nearly 17 million people tuned in to see Palin, and were treated to Adele's beautiful voice as well. When Adele first saw Palin on the set, she thought she was *SNL* alum Tina Fey doing her Palin impression. That particular episode got *SNL* its best ratings in fourteen years, so it really helped introduce Adele's music to the American public.

The day after Adele performed "Chasing Pavements" and "Cold Shoulder" on *SNL*, *19* rose to the top on iTunes charts. It reached 11 on *Billboard* 200—moving up thirty-five places from the week prior. This was great news to Adele. She was making it big in America!

Just Rewards

Adele stayed busy, not only writing music, but also racking up awards. She was the first recipient of the 2008 BRIT Awards Critics' Choice. The pretty British singer was also named the number-one predicted breakthrough act of 2008. This award is based upon polls done by the music critics at the British Broadcasting Corporation (BBC).

Also in 2008, Adele was nominated for a 2008 Mercury Prize award. It's an award given based on what can be achieved in music. Q Awards nominated her for Breakthrough Act, and Music of Black Origin nominated her for Best UK Female. She won and took home an Urban Music Award for Best Jazz Act.

The Recording Industry Association of America certified *19* as gold in February 2009. This meant it had sold 500,000 copies in the United States. By July 2009, it had sold 2.2 million copies worldwide. Also in 2009, at the 51st Annual Grammy Awards, Adele took home Best New Artist and Best Female Pop Vocal Performance. She also received nominations for Record of the Year and Song of the Year.

Adele was nervous about attending the Grammys. "When I got there, I felt so out of place," she told CBS Arts Online. "It was really, really amazing. Everyone was walking around, like it was really normal . . . . Out in the wings, it was me, P-Diddy, Neil Diamond, and Jay-Z. We were all just there. I got to my seat and Snoop Dog was there. It was the most surreal thing ever."

Adele performs "Chasing Pavements" during the 51st Annual Grammy Awards.

To honor Neil Diamond's recording career, Adele sang his song "Cracklin' Rosie" at the MusiCares Person of the Year celebration in 2009. "I tried to pull out of it at the last minute, a couple days before .. .. The last thing I wanted to do was learn another song and all his songs I knew were taken. He heard that I had been stressing about it, I cried about it and I had been really scared. He told me, 'I am so sorry I stressed you out. I didn't mean that, I just really wanted you to perform.'"

In 2009, she was also nominated for three BRIT Awards, for Best British Female, Best British Single, and Best British Breakthrough. She even received a thank-you letter from British Prime Minister Gordon Brown. The note said, "With the troubles that the country is in financially, you're a light at the end of the tunnel." Adele was delighted to hear that her music was affecting her fellow Brits in such a positive way.

Winning Big

Adele ended 2009 with a bang. She was getting lots of attention and praise. She wasn't used to that. After the Grammy wins, she began to hide out. She canceled a bunch of appearances. She grew afraid of paparazzi. Paparazzi are photographers who make money taking pictures of stars. They follow famous people everywhere they go. She told *People*, "I couldn't walk down the street without the paparazzi chasing me. I was really frightened." Adele was afraid of losing her loyal fans and record deal.

She always just wanted to make music and sing. After she realized that fans and fame came along with that, she learned to accept the attention and popularity to be able to do something that she loved doing.

Early 2010 brought a Grammy nomination for Best Female Pop Vocal Performance for "Hometown Glory." Her song "My Same" hit the German singles chart in April, following a performance by a contestant in a countrywide talent show.

ADELE!

Adele wins the Best New Artist award at the 51st Annual Grammy Awards in 2009.

Adele's version of Bob Dylan's "Make You Feel My Love" was featured on *The X-Factor*, putting it back up on the UK singles chart. It came in at number four. In June 2010, at Country Music Television's awards for Artists of the Year, country and former pop singer Darius Rucker and Adele performed a duet to Lady Antebellum's "Need You Now." Although they did not know it at the time, they would be nominated for a CMT Music award for this performance later in the year.

Changes

After living together for nearly a year, Adele and her boyfriend broke up. It wasn't fun for her anymore. While recording songs for her new album *21*, Adele found out he had started seeing someone else. This hurt her very much. She put these feelings into her lyrics.

When her album *21* was released, it had a very different sound from *19*. Hits from this album included "Rolling in the Deep," "Someone Like You," "Set Fire to the Rain," "Rumour Has It," and "Turning Tables." The new album had a more adult and country sound. She had her U.S. tour bus driver to thank for that. He played country and Nashville music while driving her around on her U.S. *19* tour. She told *Spin* magazine, "He listened to all this amazing country music and we'd rock out late at night .... listening to Rascal Flatts. It was really exciting for me because I never grew up around [that music]."

Adele, right, performs with Darius Rucker at the taping of the CMT Artists of the Year television special.

Adele arrives at The O2 Arena in London for the Brit Awards 2011.

Troubled Voice

The Adele Live tour came to the United States to promote *21*. It was great news! The tour sold out in North America. But it was bad timing for Adele. She had to cancel the 2011 ten-city U.S. tour.

She had a vocal-cord hemorrhage. This happens when the vocal cords are overused. They become swollen and damaged, they are bruised. This is bad for a singer who puts so much power into her voice. Even talking can make it worse.

"I have a hemorrhage again and it is [important] that I rest and therefore won't be able to come and do these already rescheduled U.S shows which are due to start this Friday in Atlantic City. I apologize from the bottom of my heart, sincerely I do," Adele wrote in her blog.

The first week of November, she had laser microsurgery at Massachusetts General Hospital in Boston. She had to keep resting. Some people thought she wasn't resting enough. This wasn't the first time she had to cancel shows. In April 2011, she canceled U.S. shows because of laryngitis, and she cancelled UK shows in September due to a chest infection.

While she was resting her voice, *Live at the Royal Albert Hall* was released. This was a DVD from her tour. In the U.S. it debuted with 96,000 copies sold. It became the best-selling DVD of 2011! According to Nielsen SoundScan history, she was the first artist to have the year's number-one album (*21*), number-one single ("Rolling in the Deep"), and number-one music video. Nielsen SoundScan is a company that tracks record sales.

Resting her voice didn't stop Adele from taking home awards at the 2011 American Music Awards on November 20. She took home three awards, including Favorite Pop/Rock Female Artist, Favorite Adult Contemporary Artist, and Favorite Pop/Rock album. All this was for *21*!

Adele Takes a Break

"Someone Like You" and "Set Fire to the Rain" were her second and third number-one singles from *21*, respectively. This made her break even more records. She was the first artist to have an album hold three continuous number-one hits on the Billboard 200. This is a list of the 200 hottest music albums in the nation.

◄ Adele waves from the red carpet at the MTV Video Music Awards on August 28, 2011. She won four awards for "Rolling in the Deep."

In December, *Billboard* awarded her Artist of the Year, *Billboard* 200 Album of the Year, and *Billboard* Hot 100 Song of the Year for "Rolling in the Deep." She became the first female to win all three awards.

Adele had quite a year in 2011. She sold out shows and won many awards. UK sales of *21* topped Amy Winehouse's *Back to Black*. At the time, Adele was often compared to Winehouse. Adele even beat UK sales of Michael Jackson's *Thriller* album.

In December, Adele made a shocking announcement. She was taking a break from music. She needed time off before starting her third album. Rumors spread that Adele was taking four to five years off to produce another record. Some said Adele was taking time off for her love life. Other reports said she just needed a break.

And The Winner Is. . . .

When the 2012 Grammy season arrived, Adele won big! She walked away with six awards, including Song of the Year, Record of the Year, Best Short Form Music Video for "Rolling in the Deep," Best Pop Solo Performance for "Someone Like You," and Best Pop Vocal Album and Album of the Year, both for *21*. This helped her set another record. She tied Beyoncé for the most Grammy awards won by a female artist on one night!

After her great win at the Grammys, she sent her fans a message from her blog. She wanted to let them know that she decided

◀ *Adele poses with her six awards at the 54th Annual Grammy Awards. Among others, she won awards for Best Pop Solo Performance for "Someone Like You," and Best Pop Vocal Album for 21.*

not to take a break. "I [have] a few days off now, and then it's the BRIT Awards here at home and then I'm straight into the studio. BOYYAHH! 5 years? More like 5 days!"

In February, she gave an outstanding performance of her second hit off her *21* album, "Someone Like You," at the BRIT Music Awards. This song hit number one in the UK. The tune also helped her win one of two BRIT awards, plus three American Music Awards for *21*. In the United States, the album held the top position for 23 weeks between February 2011 and March 2012. Of those weeks not spent in the top spot, she only left the top five rankings once, and that was at number seven. This was longer than any other album since 1985. The previous album, in 1984 and 1985, was Prince and the Revolution's *Purple Rain* soundtrack. It lasted 24 weeks at number one. The album *21* was also certified platinum sixteen times in the UK. Platinum in the UK means an album sold 300,000 copies. Adele sold 4.8 million copies in the UK alone!

While *21* was flying high, *19* made a comeback. New fans wanted to check out Adele. Both "Rolling in the Deep" and "Someone Like You" were in the top five UK singles at the same time. Adele became the first living artist to score two hits in the top five in the UK in both the Official Singles Chart and Official Albums Chart since 1964. The last artist to do this was The Beatles.

That's not all! March 3 brought Adele some more *Billboard* milestones. She was the first solo female artist with three songs in the top ten of the *Billboard* 100 at the same time, two albums in the top five of the *Billboard* 200, and two singles in the top five of the *Billboard* Hot 100, at the same time! In fact, "Rolling in the Deep" was a huge hit. It was the biggest hit in twenty-five years.

Album Number Three

Fans wonder when they can expect a new album from Adele. In April 2012, Adele told ABC News, "I have to take a bit of time and live a little bit. There were a good two years between my first and second albums, so it'll be the same this time."

Her fans can't get enough of her music. They've listened to *21* and *19* on repeat and are anxious to see what her next album will sound like.

Adele arrives for the BRIT Awards 2012 at the O2 Arena in London on February 21.

Fans, Fame & Friends

Adele has always been known for being outspoken. She says what she feels. She doesn't care what people think about her. She's her own person! This is a great quality to have in showbiz. Most people in the music industry are so focused on looks. She accepts herself the way she is.

Many fans relate to Adele. She told *People*, "I've never wanted to look like models on the covers of magazines," said the singer, who embraces her curvy figure. "I represent the majority of women, and I'm very proud of that."

Adele has always struggled with her weight. Her weight has been up and down her whole life. She never dieted or worked out. To her, it wasn't a big deal. "My life is full of drama, and I don't have time to worry about something as petty as what I look like," she told *Rolling Stone*. "I don't like going to the gym. I like eating fine foods .... I don't make music for eyes, I make music for ears."

◀ *Adele arrives at the 54th Annual Grammy Awards on February 12, 2012.*

Time for a Change

After Adele's vocal-cord surgery, she lost weight. There were certain types of foods she just couldn't eat. She began to think deeply about her health. Due to her illnesses in 2011, she knew it was time for a change. She wanted to eat healthier and work out. But, it was for health reasons, not just to look a certain way. When a person focuses on eating better, weight loss comes naturally.

Adele gave up smoking and drinking alcohol, and she worked out with a trainer to keep her fit. She also took Pilates classes.

Pilates is a set of special exercises that help a person build strength.

Adele's New Love

Sometimes meeting the right person can change someone. Adele's new boyfriend, Simon Konecki, inspired her to work out. They even work out together. They follow a meat-free diet. They enjoy jogging with her dog, Louis, every morning.

Simon is a fellow Brit and is thirty-six years old. There's a big age difference. But he and Adele don't mind. They've been together for more than a year.

Simon once worked for a big investment company. He didn't agree with its views and left to do something different. He founded the bottled-water company Life. Now, he is the head of a charity called Drop4Drop. It brings clean water to poor countries. Because of this, friends often refer to him as "Waterboy."

Stage Fright

It's hard to believe that Adele would be afraid to perform. She worries that her fans won't like her concerts. This makes it hard for her to go out onstage sometimes.

Once she was so nervous, she snuck out a fire exit. "I'm scared of audiences . . . . I've thrown up a couple of times . . . . I just gotta bear it. But I don't like touring. I have anxiety attacks a lot," she told reporters.

It must take a lot for her to get onstage when she's that upset. To talk herself down, "I just think that nothing's ever gone horrifically wrong," she says. "Also, when I get nervous, I try to bust jokes. It does work. I [talk a lot] though."

For most people, once they actually get onstage, the stage fright goes away. But not for Adele. "My nerves don't really settle until I'm offstage," she says. "I mean, the thought of someone spending $20 to come and see me and

◄ *Adele gets stage fright before performing, but she finds the strength to perform anyway. Here she performs at the BRIT Awards 2012.*

saying, 'Oh, I prefer the record and she's completely shattered the illusion' really upsets me. It's such a big deal that people come give me their time." It frightens her that people pay so much money to come watch her, that maybe they compare her to the CD, and they will be disappointed in the concert.

Her stage fright is scary, yet, "The thing is," she said to *UK Vogue*, "the bigger the freak-out, the more I enjoy the show [in the end]."

Meet Sasha Carter

Adele once had a chance to meet Beyoncé. She was a nervous wreck. It made Adele sick to her stomach. Adele loves the singer. She's been a fan since age ten or eleven. Meeting her was such a big honor. Before meeting Beyoncé, Adele did something to calm herself down. "I went out on the balcony crying hysterically, and I said, 'What would Sasha Fierce do?' That's when Sasha Carter was born." Sasha Fierce is Beyoncé's other side or alter ego. Sasha is fun and flirty.

Adele's other side or alter ego is Sasha Carter. She now uses Sasha Carter to help push away her jittery nerves before performing. Sasha Carter is a cross between Sasha Fierce, Beyoncé's other side, and June Carter, a beloved country singer from the 1950s with a powerful personality. They are strong women to Adele. She considers them idols. What's cool is Beyoncé was so happy when she met Adele! She let Adele know how special she is to music.

◀ *Beyoncé and Adele are fans of each other! Beyoncé has even told Adele how much she likes her music.*

Her Fans

Adele makes time for her fans. She meets with them before shows and signs autographs when she is out and about.

Adele and her boyfriend were at a restaurant in Boca Raton, Florida. A waiter swore he recognized her. "I was 90 percent sure it was her," said waiter Alejandro Jimenez of a customer in sunglasses.

He remembered that she ordered maple-ginger-glazed salmon and a soda. "She looked beautiful and had a beautiful voice." He started to doubt himself. She seemed very down-to-earth. Nothing like a big star, the waiter thought. When he asked if she was Adele, the singer giggled, "No." It is possible that she didn't want to attract too much attention to herself at the restaurant. Instead, she left the answer on the bill. It was her autograph and a note, saying, "It was me!"

Celebs Are Fans Too

Everyday people aren't the only ones who love Adele. Fellow celebrities do too! In addition to Beyoncé, Madonna, the Foo Fighters, and more all adore Adele. Christina Aguilera tweeted a photo of her and Adele, "Me & Adele. 'Someone Like You' is my favorite! Beautiful to see all her fans sing it tonight! ;) love u Adele." Jessica Simpson tweeted about dancing at Adele's concert. *Glee* stars Dianna Agron and Kevin McHale have also tweeted fan messages to Adele. Madonna has told reporters that she would love to work with Adele: "I wanted her to be in the Super Bowl with me . . . . but unfortunately Adele was having throat issues."

Adele has mentioned on multiple occasions that when she met Beyoncé, she was floored when the singing diva told her that listening to Adele's music was like listening to God!

The duo The Civil Wars was lucky enough to join Adele on her tour. One half of the folk/country duo, Joy Williams, said, "Adele was really supportive of us right from the beginning. It was so good to be able to stand stage-side and watch her perform every night. Then becoming friends with her was really the icing on the cake. She's brilliant company."

As if Adele isn't awesome enough, *TIME* magazine named her one of the most 100 influential people of the year in 2012. In the magazine, singer P!nk wrote about her love for Adele. "There are a few artists in my life who I can think back and remember where I was when I first heard them. When you're so utterly moved by something that you know you'll never be the same again . . . . Her success renews hope in me that the world I live in has good taste—that we still occasionally come back to what's simple, and simply amazing. I can't wait to hear what she does next." And to think that P!nk actually inspired Adele when she was young!

Adele's Competition

Because Amy Winehouse and Adele had similar bluesy singing styles, Adele made fellow Brit Winehouse nervous. Mark Ronson, a friend of the singer, said, "I think that the Adele thing had Amy freaked out. She liked her, but Adele's success was making Amy feel upset, competitive and restless."

Singer Rihanna spoke to *UK Vogue* about the unspoken rivalry among female singers: "It'll always be a competition. That's why women are becoming so dominant in music right now. We're very competitive beings and we cannot stand to see another woman do better than us. That bothers us a lot. . . ." She added, "Really I came to the Brit [Awards] to stalk Adele. "It wasn't about the Brits, it wasn't about the performance, it was really just to see Adele again. I saw her at the Grammys—I love her."

Adele arrives at the 55th Annual Grammy Awards on February 10, 2013. She won a Grammy for Best Pop Solo Performance for "Set Fire to the Rain [Live]."

Adele Online

Adele is active on Twitter and Facebook, and writes a blog that's featured on her Web site. Her Twitter account was originally run by members of her staff. While recovering from her surgery, Adele started tweeting herself.

Her blog messages are brief. She uses it to let fans know how much she appreciates them. She has also used it to clear up rumors. When questions came up about her boyfriend, Simon, she said, "This is the first and last time I will comment on the details of my relationship with Simon. Contrary to reports and headlines in the press today, Simon is divorced and has been for four years. Everyone in our lives separately and together wish us nothing but the best, and vice versa. These are the facts. Take care and see you all in February xx."

Adele goes out of her way to help people. She does a lot for charity. One of her first fund-raisers took place in October 2007. Adele played backup acoustic guitar for singer Will Young. This charity concert helped MENCAP Little Noise Sessions, at London's Union Chapel. The charity helps people with learning disabilities. At the time, Adele's used her Myspace fame to raise money. Fans had started to become interested in her sound. This was one of her first public performances.

In July 2009, Adele helped a charity auction called Keep a Child Alive. She bought a commissioned painting by Stella Vine. The painting cost Adele $12,500. This event helps African families living with

Adele supported the Keep a Child Alive Annual Black Ball benefit event in New York on November 13, 2008.

Adele performed at the VH1 Divas concert in New York on September 17, 2009. ▶

HIV/AIDS. She was going to have Ms. Vine paint a picture of her and her mother.

In September 2009, Adele performed for the VH1 Divas event at the Brooklyn Academy for Music. This concert raised money for the Save the Music Foundation. Save the Music helps promote musical education in American public schools.

Adele's Favorite Cause

In addition, Adele's tour rider provides for her favorite charity. A tour rider is a list of things a singer requests before each show. This often consists of special snacks and drinks. In Adele's case, she insists that any person receiving a free ticket to her concert donates at least twenty dollars to SANDS. SANDS is a UK charity that provides support for families that have lost a child during or closely after birth. SANDS stands for Stillbirth and Neonatal Death Society.

This means anyone on the guest lists must donate. When people receive free tickets, they can pay up front, or pay when they pick up their tickets. On the night's free ticket list, it says whether people have already donated or not. This is so the people who issue the tickets know whom they need to collect money from. At the end of the night, Adele's tour manager gets the funds, along with a list of the donations. During her UK tour, Adele's fans raised $13,000. With the kickoff of her U.S. tour, Adele let her American fans know about what the UK fans had provided.

Adele's Charity Sampler

Every year, Minneapolis radio station KTCZ puts out a charity album. It includes songs from top bands and singers who perform at the station. This helps the station raise lots of money that helps Minnesota-area charities.

In late 2010, Adele performed "Someone Like You" live during a station visit. The radio station was so proud to be able to include her song on its annual charity CD, *Cities 97 Sampler: Live From Studio C: 23*. At first KTCZ wasn't sure whether it would get Adele's permission. When the station did, it rejoiced! KTCZ knew fans would love it.

Other artists on the album were Florence + the Machine and Mumford & Sons. The album benefits different organizations each year. The funds raised helped 38 local groups through the sales of the 2010 release.

The album sampler always sells out. It's only available at local Target stores in the Minneapolis, Minnesota, area. It sold out of all copies on the morning of November 17. That was the day it was released. The CD raised $800,000 for Minneapolis charities. Because of the type of recording it was, only 33,000 copies were made. This has to do with label restrictions on charity CDs. Because it sold so many copies in a single day, *Cities 97 Sampler: Live From Studio C: 23* debuted at No. 12 on the *Billboard* chart on December 3. It also came in at No. 1 on *Billboard*'s Folk Albums chart.

Helping Drop4Drop

Adele's current boyfriend, Simon Konecki, has helped inspire her to improve the lives of others. His charity helps provide clean drinking water to Third World, or extremely poor, countries. In the future, Adele may travel to Africa with Konecki on one of his trips to help more people.

On December 4, 2011, Adele tweeted, "Right! It's me! I will start tweeting if 10k of u start following @drop4drop & their trip to India this wk. It's a wonderful charity. Go! A xxx." Although there was a Twitter account in her name, she was going to tweet more often for her fans, on this condition.

One day later, on December 5, she tweeted, "....That was quick! Thank U! I'm in bed, watchin' Gladiator, eatin an apple. Here's a pic of me & Queen B [Beyoncé] last wk in NYC! X."

Amnesty International Tribute Album

In February 2012, Adele and eighty other artists recorded an album for Amnesty International. Amnesty International was turning fifty years old! This organization helps protect human rights. To celebrate, it released a tribute album called *Chimes of Freedom*.

The album consists of Bob Dylan hits sung by different artists. Bob Dylan is a folk-rock musician big in the music industry for more than fifty years. He has supported Amnesty International for a long time. The tribute album includes four CDs of songs, one of which is Adele's version of "Make You Feel My Love."

Adele's Career Future

Adele has been busy touring, recovering from throat surgery, raising money for charities, and building a loving relationship and family of her own. Although her current life is very hectic, she's also thinking about her future.

During an interview with the French radio station NRJ, Adele said, "There'll be a new song probably coming out at the end of year [2012]." She added that it may be a longer wait for a whole album. "I have to write another record," she explained.

"If I didn't write my own songs, I'd be out next week with a new album. But because I write my own songs I have to take time, and live a little bit." She said, "It was a good two years before my first and second albums, so it'll be the same this time."

Adele tries to take her success in stride. "You know, I never, ever expected the success of my first album, either, let alone how many records this one's sold," she said. "So I don't think I'll ever feel the pressure for my next record to be as big as the last

Adele cowrote "Skyfall" with Paul Epsworth for the twenty-third movie in the Bond franchise, *Skyfall*.

one, because I know it's not really possible, and what happened with this one is very rare anyway." The song that Adele hinted at was the title song of the James Bond film *Skyfall*, which was released in October 2012.

While touring in America, Adele checked out different styles of music. She especially grew fond of rockabilly, bluegrass, and country. She loves the lyrics and melodies! She told a British newspaper she hopes to spend time in Austin, Texas, or Nashville, Tennessee, to learn more about the country music scene. This could mean a future country music album from Adele!

Settling Down

Although Adele is truly passionate about making music, she told *People* magazine she'd love to be a mom by age thirty.

That happened sooner than fans thought! "I've got some news," she blogged on June 29, 2012. "I'm delighted to announce that Simon and I are expecting our first child together. I wanted you to hear the news direct from me. Obviously we're over the moon and very excited but please respect our privacy at this precious time. Yours always, Adele xx"

US magazine reported in early July 2012 that Konecki will be proposing to Adele soon. As for a big wedding, Adele would prefer "a low-key affair where her mother gives her away."

ADELE!

The couple has been keeping details of their personal life under wraps. In late August 2012 photos emerged in *Life & Style* magazine showing Adele out and about in London. The magazine also shows Adele wearing what some believe is a wedding ring. An unnamed source reported attending Adele's quiet wedding. A day after the magazine hit stands, Adele sent a tweet on August 30, 2012, saying, "I'm not married."

But the couple did welcome a son into their little family unit. On October 19, 2012, Angelo James Konecki entered the world.

Adele performs "Skyfall" at the 85th Annual Academy Awards Ceremony. The song was nominated, and won, the Oscar for Best Song.

Adele's life sure has changed since fans heard her first single. Only time will tell what Adele's career will be like now that her personal life has changed so much.

Further Info

Books

Krohn, Katherine. *Adele*. Farmington Hills, Mich.: Greenhaven Press, 2013.

Newkey-Burden, Chas. *Adele: The Biography*. London: John Blake, 2012.

Shapiro, Marc. *Adele: The Biography*. New York: St. Martin's Griffin, 2012.

Internet Addresses

Adele Official Web site <www.adele.tv>

Official Twitter: <twitter.com/OfficialAdele>

Official Facebook: <facebook.com/adele>

Official Myspace: <myspace.com/adelelondon>

Index